MW01148596

Copyright © 2004 by J.

Republished March 201/.

Publisher: Valentina Antonia, LLC.

Devilish Dot is book 6.5 and the 9th installment of an ongoing serial. For maximum enjoyment, it is recommended the serial be read in order:

- The Empress' New Clothes: Book 1, Installment 1
- No Mercy: Book 2, Installment 2
- Enslaved: Book 3, Installment 3
- No Escape: Book 4, Installment 4
- "Naughty Nancy" in Strictly Taboo: Book 4.5, Installment 5
- No Fear: Book 5, Installment 6
- Dementia: Book 5.5, Installment 7
- Seized: Book 6, Installment 8
- Devilish Dot: Book 6.5, Installment 9
- Never A Slave: Book 7, Installment 10
- No Way Out: Kari – Book 8, Installment 11
- No Way Out: Dari – Book 9, Installment 12 – Coming Soon
- No Way Out: Jana – Book 10, Installment 13 – Coming Soon
- Armageddon: Book 11, The Final Installment – Coming Soon

Devilish Dot

TREK MI Q'AN: BOOK 6.5

By Jaid Black

Chapter One

Rural California

Present Day

She loved sex. Lots and lots of sweaty, pumping, pounding, gloriously wicked, undeniably naughty, kinky as all hell S-E-X with a capital S for *Sex.*

It didn't matter where she was—even driving along the highway in her very unsexy clunker of a car, the mere thought of impending passion made Dorothy "Dot" Araiza's pulse race. It made her doe-brown eyes grow heavy-lidded and her legs squeeze together. It made her hands clench into tight fists and her breath catch in the back of her throat.

(Confused passersby on the interstates might have mistaken her arousal for seizures a time or two, but oh well.)

Yes, Dot loved sex. There was no denying that fact of life. It was just too bad she wasn't getting any, she thought with a snarl. Because maybe if she was, she wouldn't be sitting in her car, driving through a torrential downpour, voluntarily giving up her Friday night to sell her toys at a bachelorette party.

Dot's nostrils flared as she stepped on the gas pedal and plowed through the back roads of the one-horse bumpkin town like nobody's business. She'd never even heard of Nowhere, California, for Pete's sake! It certainly wasn't on the map. But work was work and if this Nowhere existed, well hell, she'd find it.

Dot supposed being a sex toy maker had its distinct advantages. She got to work from home. She enjoyed the thrill of invention. And, she thought on a harrumph that could rival any bah-humbug by Ebenezer Scrooge, the local charities never hit her up at Christmas for donations to the *Toyz For Tots* fund. One look at what kind of toys she made and all bets were off.

Her former shrink had once told her she loved sex so much because in her mind it was a replacement for affection. An infliction that mostly males suffered from, but which strikes the occasional female. If that was true, Dot supposed she was a human lightning rod.

She often fantasized about being swept off her feet by an extremely tall, muscular, hunky, alpha male kind of guy. He would snatch her up and gently but demandingly throw her onto her elegant pink satin bed with all its lace and ruffles. And then—oh boy and then!—he would, to be blunt, fuck the shit out of her. Oh yeah, Dot thought with a small smile, she entertained that fantasy a lot.

The problem with turning fantasy into reality was that, as much as she loved sex, Dot also had the distinct disadvantage of being rather, well—shy. Very shy, unfortunately. Wallflower shy, she thought through gritted teeth. Wallflower, hopeless, sexless, utterly pathetic kind of shy. *Arrrg!* The minute a man so much as glanced in her direction she was all babbling idiot and no action.

Dot thought back on the last time she'd almost done the horizontal mambo and couldn't help but to grimace. Henry had been far from tall, not at all muscular, and nowhere in the vicinity of being an alpha male. The extremely conservative and rather butt-ugly pharmacist with the perpetually running nose might not have been a hunk or even close to it, but he'd been able to put her at ease enough to talk to him. Not even a woman so shy as she was could continue to babble like an idiot rather than carry on a half-intelligent conversation with a man as harmless as Henry.

And so they'd gone out. Once. Twice. Three times. By the time the tenth date rolled around and the pharmacist had made no move to bed her, Dot feared they'd never get down to business and have sex. So she'd set out to seduce Henry. What a disaster that had turned out to be!

Dot had read in a men's magazine that males really go for forward women, that they love it when their woman seizes the moment and jumps their bones. If that was the case, she thought, her hands gripping the steering wheel until her knuckles turned white, the author of that column had clearly never met Henry.

She had donned that see-through, peek-a-boo, pink satin nightie of hers which perfectly coordinated with the pink satin draped across her bed. Slipping into her matching pair of high heels, she picked up "Diesel-Dirk" — the name she'd given to the 30-speed ten-inch vibrator she'd designed and patented herself — and sashayed into the living room of her modest home-cum-laboratory where Henry had been patiently waiting on her to get ready for yet another date at the local frozen yogurt parlor.

The sound of Henry blowing his nose into the stained, moist hankie that always accompanied him like an appendage didn't deter her. The fact that she was two inches taller (six inches in heels) and about twenty pounds heavier didn't matter in that moment. She let down her chestnut-brown hair from its confining bun, shook it out until it cascaded down her back in soft waves, took a deep breath as she regally thrust her chin up and breasts out, and continued her seductive walk into the living room.

"Hello Henry," Dot had breathed out in a practiced, sultry voice. Henry had stilled as she came to a halt before him, his eyes widening and his jaw dropping. His expression made her confidence falter for a brief second, but recalling an old Mae West line she plowed on determinedly. "Is that a gun in your pocket," she asked in a Marilyn Monroe whisper, "or are you happy to see me?"

His face chalk-white and his eyes unblinking, Henry had then proceeded to pull out two very used hankies from his pocket and lay them on the coffee table, his deer-caught-in-headlights expression never wavering. Dot had frowned. That hadn't been the reaction she'd been going for.

You were supposed to say you are happy to see me, idiot! Now what do I do!

Her heart began pounding against her breasts. Her brown eyes rounded in embarrassment and horror. She hesitated for a moment before taking a calming breath and regaining her original level of confidence.

Plowing onward, she took "Diesel-Dirk" out from behind her back. She smiled as she held up the long, thick, veined vibrator that was, if she did say so herself, the perfect imitation of a well-endowed African-American man's cock. "Dirk has given me pleasure beyond my wildest dreams," she said in that smoky voice she'd practiced for ages. "Let him give you pleasure, too, Henry."

What she'd meant by that statement was she wanted to use Dirk on herself for Henry's viewing pleasure. Apparently Henry had thought Dot meant to screw him up the butt with it for not even five seconds later, the pharmacist had gasped, eyes rolling into the back of his head, as he'd fainted dead away.

Arrrg!

Needless to say, the night had only gone downhill from there. She'd spent the next hour reviving and re-reviving a frightened, stuttering Henry. Within thirty seconds of being able to stand upright on two shaking feet, he'd run from Dot's house as though she'd sprouted horns and spewed green venom at him.

That, she thought, nostrils flaring and jaw tight as she drove down the back road through the pouring rain, had been the last time she'd had sex. Or almost had sex. That was four years ago now. Actual penetration with a member of the male species had last occurred four years before that.

The memory of *that* night was even worse than the Henry fiasco.

"Men suck!" Dot wailed into the night, yelling at everybody and nobody. "Who needs you anyway. I've got my toys!"

And oh boy did she have toys. If there was one thing Dot knew she could do better than anybody else, it was create the perfect sex toys for sexually frustrated females. Being one of those women, well, she'd managed to turn her hobby into a full-time job.

There was "Freddy-The-Fish", a male mouth that could suck a woman blind. "Cum-Hither-Kenny", a 20-speed vibrator with interchangeable heads that could do everything but make you breakfast. And, of course, there was good ole Dirk—still her most popular seller. Dirk could not only make you scream like a banshee in heat, but he was also capable of screwing you—hands free!—when mounted on a special mechanism she'd designed solely for the purpose of a woman being able to get off without having to hold the vibrator steady in her hands.

Dot reached over to the passenger seat and affectionately petted Dirk on the crown of his glorious black head. "I just want to get this damn bachelorette party over and done with," she muttered, "then me and you will go home and have a little fun."

Who needed a real man, Dot decided on down-turned lips. She had Dirk. And Kenny. And — and...

Shit!

Dot screamed as a bolt of lightning illuminated the nighttime sky and cracked down in front of her car, effectively scaring the daylights out of her. Reacting instead of thinking, she veered a sharp left and before she knew what had happened her small sedan was in a flat-spin on a rainy, muddy back road.

"Oh my God!" Dot cried out, her heart racing and her eyes wide. She couldn't get control of the car. "Somebody help me!"

It was too late. She espied the tree a moment before the sedan made impact.

Her eyes rolling back and slowly flickering shut, she saw a flash of white and then nothing else.

Chapter Two

Hunting Grounds of the Zyon Pack
Planet Khan-Gor ("Planet of the Predators")
Seventh Dimension, 6078 Y.Y. (Yessat years)

Two crimson eyes flew open. Air rushed into depleted lungs, his concaved, translucent silver chest rapidly expanding to its total musculature and size. Deadly fangs exploded from his gums. Lethal claws and talons shot out from his fingers and toes.

She is near…

He had been cocooned for one hundred earth years, his body and mind in *gorak* — the Khan-Gori term for "the sleep of the dead". *Gorak* comes every five hundred Yessat Years and occurs between each of a Barbarian's seven lives. Five hundred and one Yessat Years he had spent without *her*, without the one. He mayhap ended his first life in defeat of finding her, but his second life was about to commence —

Vaidd Zyon could feel her, could sense her, could smell her. He took a slow, deep breath, nostrils flaring and eyes briefly closing, as he inhaled her scent.

It *was* her.

His Bloodmate.

He had evolved in *gorak*. Stronger. Deadlier. More ferocious than ever he was in his first life. 'Twas time to begin his second lifetime.

Every day, every hour, every second of the five hundred and one Yessat Years he'd spent without her had been akin to the blackest abyss. No sense of hope. No sense of joy. No reason to wish to evolve in *gorak* and begin the next five hundred years without the one who had been born that she might complete him. Many a day Vaidd had felt like ending it—forever.

But his pack needed him. Verily, he was his sire's heir apparent. And so he'd carried on. Grim. Lethal. Merciless. But he'd carried on.

Vaidd took another deep breath and, once more, inhaled the scent of his Bloodmate. She was close. Very close.

The beating of his heart stilled for one angry, possessive moment when his senses confirmed something else:

She was not alone. Other males drew near.

A low growl rumbled in his throat until it turned into a deafening roar. In an explosion of violence, hunger, possession, and desire, Vaidd burst from his cocoon and shot into the air, his twelve-foot wings expanding on a predator's ruthless cry. The instinct to return to his pack was overridden by the more primal need to track his Bloodmate—and kill any male that might touch her.

Her scent was strong, intoxicating. Bewitching. She *would* be his and no other's.

She belonged to him.

* * * * *

Dot's eyelids blinked in rapid succession as she slowly, groaningly, came to. Her forehead wrinkled in incomprehension as she glanced around. "Well hell's goddamn bells," she muttered. "Where in the world am I?"

What a night! she thought tragically. Turning off the engine, she opened the door of her car and arose from the driver's seat. The rain must have ended and brought a thick fog with a cold front in its stead, for she could barely see anything at all and felt so chilled to the bone that it was as if she'd woken up in the middle of the Arctic.

Frowning, she narrowed her eyes and ran her hands up and down her goose-pimpled arms, trying to make heads or tails of her location. But the fog was thick. She couldn't see anything at all other than what was in the immediate vicinity of her car. Not even with the headlights still shining off into the distance. What she thought the oddest, however, was that the tree she had collided with was no longer anywhere to be seen. But she'd definitely struck it...

Immediately noting that the oak she'd made impact with had left a highly noticeable dent in the driver's side door, she angrily slammed the thing shut and harrumphed. Feeling in true drama-queen form, she lifted the back of her hand up to her forehead and sighed.

Great! This is just terrific! I haven't had almost-sex in four years, actual sex in eight years, I spent my Friday night driving through a horrible rainstorm in the middle of nowhere trying to find Nowhere...and now on top of everything else, my insurance premium will go through the roof!

A lesser woman wouldn't be able to pull herself together, she thought on a sniff. A lesser woman would come undone.

Dot decided she was a lesser woman.

A warbled cry of anger, frustration—no doubt partially sexual in origin!—and dismay began in her belly, gurgled up to her throat, and exploded from her mouth in a shrill, shrieking cry. She kicked the door in three times for good measure with the toe of one of the black high-heeled shoes she wore. (The ones that perfectly coordinated with her pink suit ensemble, if she did say so herself.) Might as well. The damn door would need fixed anyway!

That accomplished, she screamed again, this time longer and louder. She jumped up and down like a mad jack-in-the-box as she shrieked, fists tight and nostrils flaring. Her hair came undone out of the tight bun she'd had it coiled in, but it didn't matter. Her tantrum was making her feel better. Much better, in fact.

A low growl pierced the quiet of the night. And then another. The growls sounded as if off from a distance, but growing closer by the millisecond.

Dot immediately shut-up. She ceased jumping. Her ears perked up and her eyes widened as she looked around.

Nothing.

The fog was so thick and all-encompassing that she couldn't see anything. And the growling had just altogether stopped — practically as soon as it had begun. She swallowed a bit roughly, wondering to herself if this was what people meant by the old colloquialism, "the quiet before the storm".

Dot hastily arrived at the conclusion that she didn't want to know.

Deciding she could finish up being a lesser woman later — like in the safety of her home! — the sex toy maker determined it would, perhaps, be in her best interests to get the hell out of dodge. Like now.

What a night! What a night! What a night!

Throwing open the door of her gray sedan, Dot quickly scurried into the vehicle, slammed the dented thing shut, and locked all the doors. Her eyes still wide, she nervously glanced around to try and ascertain if any wild animals were drawing near.

The growls. They are getting closer…

Her heartbeat picking up in tempo, she mentally chastised herself for reacting like a scared ninny while simultaneously turning the key and revving up the engine. No wild animal could get into a locked car! She knew that, yet an eerie feeling persisted just the same. She felt as if she was being— well…hunted.

No doubt her imagination, but she supposed it was best to err on the side of caution.

"Come on, Dot," she mumbled to herself. "Calm down. You can do this."

Problem was, the fog was as thick as clichéd pea soup. No matter how hard she squinted, she couldn't make out where she was let alone where she was going.

The eerie feeling grew, swamping her senses. She began to drive slowly, aimlessly, forward.

Light ahead! There is light just up ahead!

Dot stepped harder on the gas pedal, determinedly driving toward the faint illumination she could just barely make out in the distance. A small, brief smile of relief shown on her lips. The light was red—it had to mean a traffic signal or something of that nature. Civilization!

But as she drove out of the all-encompassing fog and into the dark, yet visible world that awaited her, it wasn't civilization that greeted her. At least not any sort of civilization she'd ever seen.

Dot's heart stilled as she loosed up on the gas pedal and came to a jarring stop. Dumbfounded, her jaw dropped. Her mind raced, inducing dizziness.

Well, Dorothy, you aren't in Kansas anymore. What the...?

Ice-capped mountains with razor-sharp tips surrounded her on all sides. It was cold here, so terribly, hypothermia-inducing frigid. Her current location seemed to be in a semi-forested valley of sorts between two of the mountains. *Translucent silver trees??* And the red illumination—

Dot gasped as she looked up. Her doe-brown eyes rounded to the shape of the four crimson moons she was gaping up at. Four moons. Four RED moons!

Blinking out of the trance-like state that had engulfed her, she held a palm to her forehead and whimpered. Either she was in a coma in some intensive care unit having one hell of a delusional dream or that last orgasm Dirk had given her had blown her mind—literally.

"Wake up, Dot," she whispered, her unblinking eyes staring up at the four crimson moons. "This isn't happening."

A lightning-fast movement caught her attention from out of her peripheral vision. Frightened, her heart skipped a beat as her head whiplashed to the right to see what that movement had been caused by. She sucked in a breath.

A man. A *naked* man. A naked man with…with…pearly white skin, black eyes, and a—holy shit! He/It had a tail!

Dirk—arrg! What have you done to me?

And then there was another. And another. And another. And another.

Dot's heart slammed in her chest as five of these…these— things—had her small, gray sedan surrounded. All five looked hungry, practically drooling as they took in the sight of her.

They wanted to eat her, she hysterically thought. They were gazing at her like sushi.

"Oh my God!"

Screaming, Dot floored the gas pedal in an effort to outrace the creatures. Beads of perspiration broke out on her forehead and between her breasts as she frantically drove to anywhere.

Faster! Faster!

She drove aimlessly forward, not caring where the path led to so long as it didn't lead to any more of those things. But the men-beasts were bone-chillingly fast. Taking to all fours, they followed her. And—*oh God!*—caught up with her. Eighty miles an hour and they had caught up to her!

Dot's throat issued a final blood-curdling shriek for help as the creatures attacked the car, one jumping onto the hood and hissing while another pulled off the driver's side door to the sedan on a hungry growl.

Help me! Oh God—somebody help me!

Chapter Three

It didn't take the creatures long to overpower her. The car veered and swerved, Dot's mind too hysterical to scream, too frightened to do anything but try and regain control of the sedan.

This isn't happening! What are these things?

Men with tails. Black, fathomless eyes, white skin, hugely aroused dicks, and…tails! Out of all the horror and incredulity of the situation, it was the tails that she couldn't seem to work past. They looked like something out of an extremely weird (but highly creative) writer's imagination.

The creature that had managed to pull the driver's side door clean off the hinges was the biggest of the bunch. Huge, in fact. He had to stand in the vicinity of six and a half to seven feet tall. And sweet lord did he look hungry. Oh God! She didn't even want to contemplate what would happen to her if the beast-man managed to get her out of the sedan. Sushi-city.

Not even ten seconds later, nightmare became reality when, on a growl, the leader of the pack of creatures snatched

Dot straight out of the car and into his awaiting arms. Screaming, she paled to a shade of white that could almost rival that of the beast-man's coloring.

"Let me go!" she cried, tears welling in her eyes as she beat her comparatively tiny fists against his naked chest. Blood pounded in her ears. Her heart was racing so fast she felt close to hyperventilating. *"OhmyGodOhmyGodOhmy –"*

Dot let out a yelp as the creature let her drop to the ground and onto her butt. She quickly shuffled up to her knees, her eyes round, her long, light brown hair tangled and disheveled.

"Please," she whimpered, her teeth chattering. "Don't kill me." She was freezing cold, but the adrenaline kept her insides warm. From somewhere deep down inside she found the courage to look up, to meet the leader of this pack of things in the eye. He didn't seem to comprehend what she was saying—or care to understand it. His pupil-less black gaze made it impossible to determine that; it was the strange way he'd cocked his head that had made her realize he couldn't understand a word she'd said. And yet again, against all hope, she softly begged, "Please…"

Within the blink of an eye, all five of the creatures were on her, forcing her to her feet and tearing at her clothes. She tried to run, but again they pounced, easily catching her and eagerly ripping her pink suit and undergarments from her body until she was totally naked. The beast-men dragged her — kicking, naked, and screaming — from out of the icy valley and into a nearby cave.

"Help meeeeeee!" she wailed. *"Please somebody help meeeeeeee!"*

Fear the likes of which Dot had never before known engulfed her. Either these things wanted to rape her or they'd shredded her clothes to bits because it made devouring her flesh easier. Each scenario — or worse *both* scenarios — were equally distressing.

Her heartbeat raced so fast that dizziness consumed her. Perspiration once again broke out on her forehead and between her breasts. Ice-cold terror lanced through her as the five male creatures forced her to the ground and pinned her to it.

Earlier in the evening, Dot had succumbed to fainting because she'd experienced what she assumed was a temporary concussion. This time she thankfully, mercifully, fainted out of fear. Her last memory before unconsciousness took over was of her legs being harshly spread apart...and of a male head diving between her legs. Of all the places to dine on her flesh—

Just let me pass out! Oh thank you, God, for letting me faint…

* * * * *

Vaidd Zyon heard his Bloodmate's screams echo throughout the mountains. Anger and possessiveness, mingled with terror at the thought of losing his *vorah* before he'd even found her, made his already swift wings swoop up and down all the faster. A merciless growl rumbled up from his throat, his fangs and talons visible and ready to kill.

He could not lose her—would not lose her. Without her…

He chose not to contemplate it. There was, for any evolved male of learned dimensions, but one. Only *one* female who could complete him, who could bare his offspring, whose mind and soul could meld with his.

'Twas said the warriors of Trek Mi Q'an knew naught but darkness and hopelessness without the finding of their mate. Verily, a Khan-Gori male knew seven lifetimes whereas a warrior knew but one—'twas naught worse than seven lifetimes spent in darkness and defeat.

His Bloodmate was still several hundred miles off. It could take a few hours to reach her. Mayhap she'd encountered a sentinel and found herself at its mercy. Mayhap—

Vaidd frowned when his acute senses picked up the scent of the males causing his *vorah* to screech. Verily, he couldn't fathom her fright. 'Twas but a pack of harmless, hungry male yenni! Why fear weak creatures such as those? It made no sense.

Unless...

Vaidd's heart all but stopped for a moment when he realized his Bloodmate was not of this galaxy, not even of this dimension. He'd been so intoxicated with need and aroused by her scent that it never once occurred to him 'twas the scent of a female primitive bewitching him. This explained his Bloodmate's fear of the yenni. She harbored no knowledge of what they were or of how they fed.

His already aroused cock swelled impossibly harder, longer, and thicker. He had heard tales of what 'twas like to bed a primitive. Verily, a male he knew from another pack had claimed one as his Bloodmate. So heady were the tales that before Vaidd had gone into the sleep of the dead, he'd been told by members of his own pack that they were planning a scouting party to primitive, first-dimension earth to look for their *vorahs*.

'Twas said a primitive female could nigh unto suck a Barbarian blind—and ruthlessly fuck him in the bed furs. 'Twas also said that, unlike females of this dimension, primitives were harder to tame.

Vaidd absently licked his fangs as he considered the reality that was his. Five hundred and one Yessat Years he'd spent without his one. But the gods and goddesses had smiled down upon him whilst he was in *gorak*.

A primitive. A female primitive.

And she was *his*.

* * * * *

Dot gasped, semi-regaining consciousness on a hard orgasm.

"Dirk?" she whimpered, groggy eyelids fluttering open as her breathing grew labored. She moaned as her large nipples hardened, the areolas jutting up into stiff, pink points.

No—not Dirk. Freddy-The-Fish. Yes. Yes, of course.

Duh! she thought, her eyelids fanning shut on a dreamy smile. How could she have not recognized the realistic feel of the very cunnilingus toy she'd created with her own two hands?

Slurp. Slurp. Slurp. Sluuuuuuuuurrrrrrrrp.

Dot frowned. She couldn't recall Freddy ever being able to make sounds with his mouth. A worthy idea, she mentally conceded. Perhaps the newer model she was working on could...

She stilled. Memories jolted through her.

A car crash. Fog. Icy mountains. Bone-chilling coldness. Four crimson moons. Man-things with big dicks — and tails!

Her eyelids flew open on a soft cry, her brown gaze traveling down her body — and between her legs. "Holy shit," she mumbled.

They were down there. All five of those...those — *things*. And they were lapping at her pussy juice like it was a meal or something.

Her heart began to race. Her breasts heaved up and down.

On a groan, Dot slapped a palm to her forehead. "I've lost it!" she wailed. She grimly wondered if the losing of one's mind was a fate common to any woman who hadn't been almost-laid in four years and totally laid in eight. She had given up on finding a man so now her delusional brain was creating fictional males for her — five of them no less!

But what the hell is with the tails!?

Dot decided that *that* particular aspect of the delusion had to be Freudian in nature. Perhaps she shouldn't have dumped her shrink so quickly after all.

But this feels so real…

A low, warning growl issued from one of the males. Dot's forehead wrinkled. She recognized that male. He was the one she had, for some reason, thought of as the leader of the pack of creatures when she'd first encountered them.

And, indeed, he was. At his growl, the other four males whimpered and scampered away from Dot's body while the biggest of the beast-men continued lapping at her pussy, licking up all her juices. Her breathing grew impossibly heavier. Torn between fear and arousal, she didn't know what to do. She didn't even know if this was real. It just couldn't be! It felt real, but, clearly, situations such as this one were out of the realm of every day reality and more like a perverse episode straight from *The Twilight Zone*. She half expected to hear Rod Serling's voice echo throughout the cave she was being held a sexual hostage in at any given moment.

Slurp. Slurp. Slurp. Sluuuuuuuuurrrrrrrrrp.

The more juice the manimal licked up, the bigger his penis grew. Beads of perspiration broke out on Dot's forehead at the realization of it. Was he going to penetrate her now? Oh sweet lord—nooooo! She didn't want that to happen. Not even in a dream.

Get up and run! Run, Dot! This isn't a dream!

Her mind was screaming that this odd situation was real. Her psyche gave her many reasons for believing as much, but it was the stark coldness of the cavern floor that underlined the horrifying fact this was really happening. Throughout her thirty-five years she'd experienced every sort of nightmare and pleasant imagining there was to be had in the world of slumber, but never once had she been able to feel such acute tactile sensations as bitter coldness.

It was real. She didn't know the how. She didn't comprehend the why. She had no idea where she was. But this was real.

Oh God.

Dot jarred herself upright into a sitting position, her eyes wide and her heart racing. Within the blink of an eye, the other four males were growling and attacking her, bodily forcing her to her back. One of the man-beasts sat behind her and stretched her arms out high above her head so that her breasts were thrust upward, a sexual offering to the others. Her pink nipples stabbed up into the air from a combination of cold and the orgasm she'd been awoken to.

"Stop it!" she screamed, hysteria rising. She struggled with everything she had in her, all to no avail. "Please — please let me go!"

A set of male lips found one erect nipple. His tongue snaked out, latched around it, and drew it in to the heat of his mouth. She whimpered. A second male mouth found her other nipple, again, making her whimper. By the time a third tongue touched her, the skinny, silky muscle invading her anus, she cried out, half moaning and half whining. God help her, she didn't know if the sound was from fright, arousal, or both.

The fifth male — the alpha male of this horde of creatures — stared at her splayed open pussy. He practically salivated as he watched it puff up and glisten. But he did nothing. Just sat there and stared at it, his fathomless black eyes in an almost trance-like state.

Dot groaned as the tongue in her anus fully penetrated her. It slid back and forth as if fucking her, slowly and with a sensuousness that was at odds with the force of the situation. She'd never felt anything like it before. She was frightened beyond comprehension, yet couldn't keep from moaning any sooner than she could keep from breathing.

The mouths at her breasts suckled her erect nipples harder. She gasped, her back involuntarily arching. That only served to thrust her breasts up like an offering, giving the creatures better access to her stiff nipples. They suckled them like lollipops, never tiring, each lick seemingly better to them than the last. The tongue in her anus kept up its slow, steady rhythm, driving her insane with a bizarre combination of terror and desire.

"Oh God," Dot breathed out. "Please...stop...stop...stop."

Her voice trailed off, fading more with each spoken word. Her entire body felt like it was on fire, being consumed by erotic, if perverse, flames. The creatures kept up their sucking, licking, and stroking. The smallest of the men-beasts continued to hold her hands high above her head so she couldn't move. All she could do was lie there and take it, her body being worked into a tight pitch of sensual nerve endings and sensations.

Her heart slammed against her chest. Her ragged breaths turned into steady moans. She tried to twist and turn, to escape the erotic ache being forced upon her, but the more she struggled the more intense the sexual longing became. The creatures sucked harder.

And harder. And harder.

The alpha male went in for the kill.

On a low growl, the leader of the creatures buried his head between Dot's thighs. She shouted out a warbled cry as his long, silky tongue stroked her clit. She screamed when his mouth latched around the sensitive piece of flesh and suckled it hard. He showed her no mercy, knowing as he had to that she was close to coming. He slurped her clit into his mouth over and over, again and again. Faster and faster and—

Dot burst into a million proverbial pieces, a violent orgasm ripping from her belly. *"Oh God,"* she gasped, blood rushing to her face, nipples, and cunt. Her nipples poked up so high it was at once pleasurable and painful. Her breathing was so ragged she feared fainting again. *"Oh God."*

Then, just like before, all five of the creatures scampered between her legs to lap at the flow of her juices with their long, skinny tongues. And, again just like before, the warning growl of the alpha male scared the others off.

The alpha male dined on her—literally—alone. He lapped up every bit of juice there was to extract from Dot, milking her like the teat of a damn cow. His cock grew in size and fierceness with each and every drop he took from her. She worried once again if now was when it—the thing—meant to rape her.

It didn't.

The sexual process repeated itself. Again. And again. And again. Early morning darkness became twilight and twilight became sunrise.

By the time Dot reached brutal orgasm number five, she had no juice left in her to give. The creatures must have realized as much for just that quickly they withdrew and she was forgotten.

Feeling weak and depleted, Dot sat up, open-jawed, as she warily watched the pack of beast-men scurry out of the cave they'd drug her into. Just like that. Weird. They'd made her come five times and then they left. *They are men all right!* There was no other word for the incredulousness of the situation other than weird.

She must have sat there a solid five minutes trying to make heads or tails of what had just transpired — and why. No answers were coming.

Snapping out of the daze that had engulfed her, Dot blinked and, feeling weak-kneed, dragged herself up to her feet. Her clothes had been torn to shreds. Without five warm hands, bodies, and tongues keeping her body temperature up, the bitter coldness of the environment began seeping into her bones.

She was drained of energy, but she recognized that she needed to get out of the cave and into her car—and as far away from this weird place as possible. A gnawing, gut-wrenching feeling inside told her escape from this bizarre world wouldn't be so easy as that, but there had to be a way. She just needed to find it.

Where there is an in, she mentally reminded herself as she walked on wobbly legs toward the cavern entrance, there is also an out. Figuring out where she was and how she'd gotten here wasn't nearly as important as finding that out.

Naked and shivering, Dot slowly, cautiously, crept out of the concealment of the cave. Her eyes nervously darted back and forth as she looked for her car.

Chapter Four

There it was. The sedan.

Shaky legs or no shaky legs, Dot dashed from the semi-protection the cave offered and toward her car as fast as her feet would carry her. Her large breasts bobbed up and down so fast that it hurt, but she didn't care. She just wanted to get inside her car.

And as far away from this horrible place as possible.

"Almost there," she panted, running faster. She could hear the crunch of freshly fallen snow under her feet but paid it no attention. She held her arms against her chest to keep her breasts from bobbing every which way. "Keep moving."

It was bitterly cold, snow and ice surrounding her on all sides. Her feet were so chilled they were numb, her skin a shield of goosebumps. She ignored everything, concentrated only on getting to her sedan.

By the time Dot reached the car, her breathing was so heavy and her teeth chattering so badly that she felt certain she was going to die. She whimpered when she came face to face with the non-existent driver's side door, only then recalling that it had been torn off the hinges by one of those creatures.

And just what were those creatures? she asked herself for what felt like the hundredth time as she got in the car, revved up the engine, and turned the heater to full blast. She'd never encountered anything like them, had never even heard any bigfoot-esque urban legends regarding men-beasts that resembled those ones. Men-beasts who dined on a woman's juices no less! It was totally perverse. It reminded her of a sci-fi series she'd once read that had been penned by a weird (but highly creative) author of erotic romances. The only difference between that series and this reality in so far as she could tell was there would be no hero to save the day. Getting out of this situation was completely up to Dot.

The blast from the heater felt so good that she closed her eyes for a protracted moment and breathed in deeply. The icy chill creeping in from the missing driver's side door was the only negative that kept the experience from being the nirvana that it should have been.

Thinking quickly, Dot turned off the engine, jumped out of the car and ran around to the trunk. She popped it open, pulled out a few empty garbage bags she'd thankfully been too lazy to throw out, grabbed a reel of duct tape, slammed the trunk shut, and dashed back to the inside of the sedan.

After re-revving the engine, she set to work at making a mock door that would, while not perfect, at least keep most of the bone-chilling cold outside where it belonged.

It worked. Within moments, Dot was warm, toasty, and sighing contentedly. She let herself bask in the glorious heat for a long moment before forcing herself to the task at hand — getting the hell out of dodge.

What a night! What a night! What a night!

Had she been out of harm's way at home, she would have had to dramatically recap the events she'd endured within the last several hours in order to brood over them. (She was good like that.) The martyr routine would, unfortunately, have to wait for later. Until she actually *found* home and could do said brooding safely. She was naked and shell-shocked — she wanted the hell out of here.

Putting the car into driving mode, Dot lightly pressed the gas pedal with her foot and drove back toward the thick forest of icy trees that had once engulfed her. It was the only rational direction she could think to take. Somewhere in those trees lay the key to Alice getting out of the rabbit hole and back to a reality where the rules, if imperfect, at least made some modicum of sense.

"Please, God," Dot muttered to herself, "let me find home." Suddenly smog, clogged California traffic, and actors-turned-governors didn't seem like such a bad thing. She'd take them, hands down, over men with tails and pupil-less black eyes any day of the week. "I promise to go to mass again," she said tragically, her voice squeaky. "And I'll quit sending Henry hate SPAM to his email address." (Maybe.) "And I'll—"

Her bartering with God came to a halt. Dot slammed on the brakes. She shook her head, unable to believe what she was seeing.

Those…things. They were just off to the left. And they had another female cornered. *Oh no!*

Dot didn't know what to do or how to help the other woman. Those creatures were super fast and unbelievably strong. The last run-in with them had resulted in her driver's side door being ripped off its hinges! What could she, naked and unarmed, possibly do to help? But how could she leave another female to the same fate? What kind of a person would that make her?

Nostrils flaring, Dot's eyes narrowed into wicked brown slits as she spun the steering wheel left, floored the gas pedal and drove top-speed toward the pack of men-beasts.

Adrenaline surged through her blood. She gripped the steering wheel tightly. She felt like G.I. Jane on a mission.

Men suck! All of them! Even the ones with tails!

Feeling instant camaraderie with the pack's next victim, Dot flew toward the creatures like a NASCAR superstar. She would save this fellow female come hell or high water.

The closer she got, the more she could see of what the beasts were doing to their newest captive. Oh sweet lord…the man-beasts weren't just orally stimulating this poor woman to milk her for her juices. The leader of the pack was penetrating her — raping her! The other four held the growling, shrieking, mad-as-all-hell female down while the alpha male got his rocks off. The alpha male held up his victim's tail and penetrated her from behind, nipping at her neck and growling her into submission and…

Dot slammed on the brakes. Her jaw dropped open. The realization jarred her as much as the quick stop did:

The female had a tail, too.

Dot sat there in her sedan and stared, morbid curiosity overwhelming her, the scientific wheels in her mind spinning. Those manimals had captured Dot. The alpha male, and only the alpha male, had drank from her juices. The more he drank, the more swollen his cock had become. And then the beasts had left. And now the alpha male was—was he trying to impregnate this female of his species?

What a night! What a night! What a night!

"Oh how gross," Dot murmured. *Could this be how they mate?* "I can't believe I'm seeing this." Or that her orgasms had somehow helped this disgusting mating process along.

She slapped a palm to her forehead and whimpered. This was just too much.

Preparing to put the sedan in reverse and find her way out of this nightmare, a deafening roar pierced the icy valley, echoing throughout the mountains. The sound was so low and lethal that it sent a chill coursing down Dot's spine. It must have scared off the pack of things as well, for a mere second after the alpha male spurted inside the female of his species, all six of the creatures scampered off into the thick of the forest.

Dot might not be an aficionado at anything save inventing sex toys, but she knew when to take a cue. Whatever had issued that horrific growling sound was deadly—and no doubt a lot bigger than those already brawny creatures that had previously kidnapped her and held her hostage until they'd gotten what they wanted from her. Otherwise, they wouldn't have scampered off the way they did.

Alice, it's time to find your way out of the rabbit hole…

Putting the car in reverse, Dot swung the sedan around as fast as it could move, switched the gear to Drive, and took off like a bat out of hell. She drove toward the forest as if her life depended on it. She realized with dawning terror that it just might.

Another roar. Impossibly louder this time. He/It was getting closer.

Dot's heart slammed against her chest like a bucket of stones. She didn't know how, didn't understand why, but she knew beyond a shadow of doubt that this newer, deadlier threat was chasing her in particular. And only her.

"This is not happening!"

Another blood-curdling roar. And then he was there.

Dot's eyes widened in terror as she saw a huge, silver, winged creature descend from the heavens like an avenging angel — or demon. The closer he got, the larger he looked. "Holy shit!"

She floored the gas pedal, screaming as the realization she was being hunted by a gargoyle firmly took root…and sent a wave of terror through her that made the fright she'd experienced from the men-beasts with tails pale in comparison. This new threat was at least twice the size of the alpha male in that last pack in terms of musculature—and no doubt a thousand times more deadly.

And he—it—wanted *her*.

Vaidd could smell her fear, could sense her panic and desire to be as far away from him as 'twas possible. Verily, he wished it could be otherwise, yet he would claim her no matter what she felt, or didn't feel, for him.

The instinctual need to impregnate his female nigh unto consumed him. The scent of her sweet, sticky cunt beckoned to him, made his already erect shaft grow harder. He had to have her the soonest.

She would grow to love him. Six lifetimes they would spend together. That she feared and loathed him in this brief moment mattered naught. All that was of consequence to Vaidd was claiming what was rightfully his. And this primitive female *was* his.

The loneliness. The desolate ache that had consumed him from having spent so many Yessat Years without her. No laughter. Little joy. Grim countenance. Dead heart.

That was about to change.

Swooping down toward the odd moving mechanism his *vorah* was trying to escape from him in, Vaidd hissed in a way in which females of his species would immediately recognize meant, "you better come to me, wench, or else". His woman paid his warning growl no heed. He would have been amused were he not so coldly intent on catching her, so desperate to claim her.

Khan-Gori m'alana fey, zya. I will not harm you, little one.

He sent out the mental call, realizing she could not understand his language, but hoping she sensed the gentleness behind the message. He sent out the wave again in the tongue of his pack. *Khan-Gori m'alana fey, zya.* Mayhap her heart would understand even if her ears did not.

But still she sought to escape him. She continued moving in the metal box, shrieking words he did not understand as she attempted to thwart capture.

On a primal, territorial, "you better obey me *now*" roar rather than a warning hiss, Vaidd plunged down from the sky and landed upon the front of the metal box. His pupils narrowed and his crimson eyes flared as he bared his fangs at his *vorah*. She screamed from behind an odd, flimsy sort of window, her beautiful eyes wide with fear of him.

The metal box came to a smoking, grinding stop under Vaidd's unforgiving weight. The ensuing screams that gurgled up from his primitive woman's throat nigh unto gave his head the ache. Verily, he decided, 'twas high-pitched enough to make a lesser Barbarian wince.

Vaidd winced.

Grunting, he determined 'twas time to claim what was his, and hopefully call a halt to the near-deafening squeals. His ears were far too sensitive, his hearing too acute, for wails such as those. Growling low in his throat, he used a razor sharp fingernail to cut through the top of the metal box, and then with the mightiness of his biceps, picked it up and threw it aside.

The shrieking grew worse as his naked *vorah* tried to scoot away. He felt nigh unto dizzy from the hellish sound of it. Or mayhap that's just what he told himself so as not to feel the lovesick dunce. In truth, being this close to her, smelling the scent of his one, was so heady as to be drugging. She was trapped. She was perfect.

And she was all his.

Dot didn't know whether to faint, cry, scream, or do a combination of all three. She decided to keep screaming as she quickly glanced around for a weapon—any weapon.

Immediately ascertaining that she had nothing to protect herself with, save a few sex toys still lying in the passenger seat, she made do. Picking up "Freddy-The-Fish" and wielding him at the eight-foot gargoyle like a talisman, she blindly threw the cunnilingus toy at the giant. It struck home. Kinda.

Breathing heavily, Dot's shrieking calmed as she watched Freddy's mouth latch onto the gargoyle's cock and start sucking. The giant stilled, his red eyes slowly rolling to the back of his head.

He liked it! The inventor in Dot couldn't help but to see dollar signs light up in her eyes. Doh! She should have marketed a "Fredrika-The-Fish" toward male clients. (She made a mental note to get started on that project as soon as she escaped.)

Deciding there was no better time to try and flee into the forest than when the towering hulk was distracted, Dot subtly began to slide toward what was once a driver's side door. Realizing the garbage bags had gone the way of the car's hood, she knew her best chance at getting away was now.

The adrenaline began to pump faster, surging through her. She was naked—how could she survive in the freezing cold temperature without clothes? It didn't matter. She'd die here anyway. The fangs, claws, and talons the gargoyle was sporting told her that he probably wasn't a vegetarian.

Unfortunately, as soon as Dot began creeping towards the way out, the giant became aware of her presence again. And oh dear did he look angry. Not good.

Tearing Freddy's mouth off from around his cock with a popping sound, the huge male flung the toy away from him and growled with such loud intensity that Dot had to cover her ears. *What do I do now? God…please help me!*

More terrified than ever before, she snatched up "Diesel Dirk", stood up on the seat, and wielded the 10-inch vibrating cock like a baseball bat. "Come on!" she spat. Jaw clenching, she decided she wouldn't become sushi without a fight. "You want some of me?" she challenged. "Let's go!"

Later she would question her sanity. For now, feigning a lack of fear was all she could think to do.

Dot could have sworn she heard the gargoyle sigh. She supposed she couldn't blame him. She probably looked as formidable as a plump, juicy fish did to a hungry bear. All protein, no fear.

Her adrenaline running high, Dot aimed the baseball bat—Dirk—at the giant's torso and swung with all of her might. In a lightning-fast motion, the gargoyle snatched Dirk out of her grasp. She stilled. He licked his fangs.

Oh fuck.

"I-I really don't taste that good," Dot squeaked, shaking like a leaf in a hurricane. She tried to think of a tastier alternative than her flesh—one that might appease the giant and his no doubt voracious appetite. Thinking quickly, she fell back into the seat and popped open the glove compartment. *Snack cakes? That's it? Arrrrrg!* It would have to do.

"Here boy," she said calmly, if a bit unsteadily. Dot held up the solitary package of stale snack cakes she had left in the sedan and dangled them in front of him with a weak smile. She couldn't think of anything else to do! She'd heard of things like feeding sugar cubes to horses and fish to dolphins in order to endear one's self to the animals in question, but the subject of gargoyle snacks had never come up in parochial school. "These are r-really good," she shakily encouraged him. "T-Try one."

Her eyes round, Dot hastily licked her dry lips as she watched the giant pluck the snack cake from her grasp with a gentleness she had not been anticipating. A silver hand with five razor-sharp black claws took the gift, held it to his nose and sniffed, and then proceeded to swallow it whole, wrapper and all. The scene brought to mind a killer shark being fed a cracker—definitely not filling enough to appease.

Okay, smart one, now what?

Up until now, Dot's gaze had skittishly avoided the giant's. Shy to her grave, she supposed. But something she couldn't explain, some force beyond her understanding, told her to look him in the eyes. She did. She hesitated for a brief moment, but she did.

Crimson red eyes clashed with frightened doe-shaped brown ones. An instant calm settled over her. Words filled her mind—foreign words she didn't understand. The longer she stared at the gargoyle, the further her consciousness drifted. Away and away, a feather in a gentle wind…

Dot closed her eyes for a brief moment, a trance-like state enveloping her, engulfing every fiber of her being. When next she flicked her eyes open, she saw the giant reaching toward her, beckoning her to go to him. It felt like it was happening to somebody else.

One second she was seated in the sedan. The next she was in his leathery embrace, her arms around his neck. She swallowed a bit heavily as her gaze once again found his. She blinked several times in rapid succession, shaking the trance-like, surreal feeling off.

Dot was given no time to rethink the fact that she'd just gone into the gargoyle's arms willingly. A rumbled growl and a push up from two powerful thighs later, the giant and his captive shot up into the air and took flight, leaving all hopes of escape for Dot far behind.

Suddenly she wished she'd kept more snack cakes in the car.

Chapter Five

Wings fiercely swooping up and down, his *vorah* securely in his arms, Vaidd flew at top speed back toward the hunting grounds of the Zyon pack. The need to claim her, to mark her as his possession, was nigh unto overwhelming. His cock was stiff with aching need to sink deep inside of her sticky, tight flesh. Yet Vaidd had captured his wench in enemy territory. The instinct to protect what was his pounded inside of him as ruthlessly as the instinct to become one with her—

Verily, she was his key. His key to sanity. His only hope at escaping from the dark void within. Without her he would choose death. There would be no reason to evolve a second time when the next *gorak* came for there was but *one*.

Vaidd could sense his *vorah's* distress. He knew that she didn't understand what was happening, where they were going, or what fate would befall her. Until he could drink of her blood, and she of his, there would be no answers forthcoming for her. Verily, he had no means until the mating to communicate with her in a tongue she could comprehend.

She wasn't the only confused one for Vaidd found himself questioning just how it 'twas a primitive had found her way to Khan-Gor. Very few within his own dimension of space and time even realized that the ice-planet existed. 'Twas believed, as the elders of the packs had wanted outsiders to believe, that Khan-Gor was naught but a legend. And so it had been for millions of Yessat Years.

Vaidd found himself not caring about the how and the why. Mayhap not even his Bloodmate understood how she had come to be here. And truly, it mattered not. She was here. 'Twas all that he had a care for.

In a few minutes more, Vaidd Zyon would be firmly within the stronghold of his pack. And then, at long last, he could claim his woman for all eternity.

* * * * *

Dot held onto the giant's neck for dear life. His massive arms were securely around her middle, but she was taking no chances. Plus his leathery skin kept her naked body feeling toasty warm.

If there had been any lingering doubts but that Dot had somehow, ludicrous and insane as it sounded, been transported into another world, they were laid to rest in midair. This icy cold place was unlike anything she'd ever seen before.

The trees below, when not coated in ice, were either purple or a blackish-blue—colors rarely seen in any vegetation back on earth except for maybe flowers and the occasional eggplant. Four suns hung in the skies—they were far away—so far away that the heat they radiated couldn't penetrate the bitter coldness of the atmosphere—but they were there. Foreign, bizarre birds flew by, weird looking animals with multiple heads stampeded below...

No. Dot was most definitely not on earth.

She didn't know where they were, where they were going or, most importantly, what would happen to her once they got there. The endless scenarios swimming through her mind ranged from being dinner to becoming a gargoyle's sex slave. She didn't know which possibility was worse.

If her captor killed her quickly and waited to make a meal of her post-mortem, well, she didn't want to die but at least that was a merciful death. Now if he preferred his food fresh and still alive while eating...

She whimpered. *Sweet lord, please don't let that happen!*

Unfortunately, becoming the gargoyle's sex slave didn't seem any more appealing than being human sushi. Both ways lay torture. She could feel his stiff cock underneath her naked bottom—she was using it as a seat for goodness sake!—and lordy, lordy was his manhood huge. He made her well-endowed sex toys look like prepubescent boys. For the first time in four years, Dot grimly understood just why Henry had fainted when she'd held up Dirk. She felt a bit on the dizzy, swooning side herself. Fate, it seemed, had a perverse sense of humor.

And by the way, God, when I was fantasizing all those years about being swept off my feet by an extremely tall, muscular, hunky, alpha male kind of guy…this was NOT what I had in mind!

Apparently she should have been more specific in her platitudes to the higher power, she thought tragically. But it was too late, and she knew it.

They began to descend. Dot's gaze immediately honed in on the cave they were heading toward. She shivered, her eyes widening, as she wondered what exactly would happen to her in this cave. The memory of what had transpired in the last one was still fresh in her mind. It had only ended, after all, but a few hours ago.

Dot had no notion as to what vile plans the gargoyle had in mind for her, but one certainty was crystal clear: he had no intention of releasing her. It didn't take an educated guess to figure that much out. Not with the way he was holding onto her as if he might never get a hold of a plumper, better meal.

With a heavy heart and stoic resolution, she realized that the giant wouldn't let her escape him alive—

Ever.

* * * * *

At long last they reached the Zyon hunting grounds. Vaidd realized that a celebratory feast for his return from *gorak* most likely lay in waiting within the sanctum—the large gathering place deep within the village's innermost cavern where all ceremonial and religious gatherings of the pack occurred. His fellow Barbarians would be expecting his return from *gorak*. What they would not be anticipating, however, was Vaidd's homecoming from the sleep of the dead with his Bloodmate in tow.

That his woman happened to be a primitive...

Verily, 'twould be the talk of all Khan-Gor. There was but one other female primitive—Nancy—who dwelled within the whole of the ice-planet, and forever was her Bloodmate keeping her close to his side. Vorik took no chances that another male might wish to steal her for *vorah* theft did happen every now and again. 'Twas rare, for a true mating was what Barbarians coveted, but the depths a Khan-Gori would sink to when nearing the end of another lifetime and still without a Bloodmate...

Like Vorik, Vaidd would take no chances with his wench either. He had waited a full lifetime to find her — that he was possessive of her was an understatement for a certainty.

On a roar his people would understand announced his return from the sleep of the dead, Vaidd landed on two feet at the mouth of Zyon Rock — the entrance to the pack's village. He could feel his Bloodmate tense up, understood that she knew not what was to transpire.

They needed to mate. Their blood needed to mingle. Until it did, she would have no comprehension of his words, his pack's language. And he would have no understanding of anything she spoke to him either. But once their blood did mingle, they would be able to communicate freely. 'Twas the way of the all-knowing gods.

Setting his Bloodmate down on two shaky feet, he stood her before him. The entryway at Zyon Rock was a wee bit cold to her delicate humanoid form, yet bearable.

His cock swelled just staring at her. She was beautiful, so very perfect in every way. Long waves of hair in a hue of light brown he'd never before seen, two gorgeous eyes a deeper, richer color of the same shade. Full breasts. Long legs. Plump in all the right places.

Lifting a hand toward her in a non-threatening, slow manner, Vaidd palmed her chin and patiently waited for her to meet his gaze. To her credit, she did — no hypnotism necessary. She was nervous, he knew, but she'd still looked up at him.

Vaidd slowly threaded his lethal black fingernails through the soft waves of her hair. He didn't smile, but his emotions were there in his eyes.

I've waited so long to find you, little one. Mayhap you fear me now, but soon you will understand that no harm shall ever come to you. Verily, you are the only one in existence who need not fear me. I will protect you with my own life.

The mental call was in his own tongue, so Vaidd realized she had no comprehension of his words. Yet he hoped her heart understood.

As his *vorah* stood there and watched, Vaidd shape-shifted from his *kor-tar* form and back to his humanoid one. His face hard and stoic, he watched his Bloodmate gasp and back away from him.

She stood there for a long while, her jaw agape, as if trying to work things out in her mind. He shape-shifted back into his *kor-tar* form, then again to his humanoid one—this time donning the clothing of his clan, that she might know her eyes were not deceiving her.

Apparently males of her species were not able to take on other forms. 'Twas the only explanation Vaidd could fathom for a moment later his wench's gorgeous eyes rolled to the back of her head…and she fainted.

Dot blinked several times in rapid succession, unable to believe what she was seeing. One second there was a gargoyle there and then the next—holy shit!—there was a man standing before her. A very, very capital B-I-G for BIG, naked man. He must have stood seven and a half to eight feet tall. His hair was a light brown with golden streaks, his eyes like molten silver. His body was heavily muscled, a jagged scar zigzagging down the right side of his torso. His cock was just as ferociously swollen now as it had been while in gargoyle mode.

No way.

She gasped, backing away. There was *no way* that…

He shifted again—back to the gargoyle. And then again—back to the man.

Now he was clothed. Sorta. His chest was bare, but he wore a black and red kilt-like skirt that stopped mid-thigh…huge, massively sculpted thighs! The dark leather boots he was sporting ended just below the knee.

Dot began feeling dizzy. Until last night she'd never fainted before in her life. Now she wondered if it was to become an average, daily event for her.

Breathe, Dot, breathe. Slow, deep breaths. Slower. Deeper. Arrrrrrrg!

Unfortunately, nothing short of a tranquilizer was likely to make her breasts stop heaving up and down. This was just too much to take in. This man, this-this…*thing*…spent part of his time looking like a wicked nightmare straight out of a B-rated horror movie and the other part of it looking like a human — an incredibly gigantic human but still a human.

And she was standing in front of him naked no less! Somehow, when he'd been a gargoyle, her state of undress hadn't much mattered; it had been like standing in the nude in front of a creature at the zoo. Not a big deal, other than the fact she was likely to become his dinner. But now her nudity bothered her — a lot.

She was a poster girl candidate for the all-American, Catholic, sexually frustrated spinster for the love of God! She invented large, vibrating penises for her pleasure because she was too shy to meet the real deal. Talking to men she didn't know could welt up her entire body with a case of nervous hives. Standing in front of one naked was not precisely a walk in the park.

Oh dear God in heaven, why hast thou forsaken me?

A prayer straight from the drama queen bible, perhaps, but Dot felt as though she had that moment of martyrdom coming to her and then some. Her first instinct was to cover up her various intimate parts with her hands as best as she could manage. She never got that far. The entire situation frayed her nerves like violin strings that had been strung so tightly they snapped at the first pluck.

Her jaw agape while she stared at the large male as though he had two heads — and for all intent and purposes he did! — Dot's brown eyes slowly rolled to the rear of her head. Stiff as a board, she plunged straight backwards.

And, yea, though I walk through the valley of the shadow of death…oh…never mind!

Arrrrrrg!

Chapter Six

Vaidd's nostrils flared as he roared in his throat, customarily acknowledging his pack members' boisterous clapping, hissing, and growling. Some shifted into their *kor-tar* form, some merely sprouted fangs and roared back at him.

His sire's eyes widened. As Vaidd strode into the sanctum, the sight of his eldest son's Bloodmate asleep in his arms was more of a triumph to him and the rest of the pack than even was Vaidd's return from *gorak*.

Their line, unlike that of so many other Barbarian packs, would go on.

Verily, Vaidd's mother had entered her fifth lifetime and his sire the seventh. The pack's matriarch was still within childbearing years, though the patriarch was not. Male Khan-Gori became sterile once they left their sixth lifetime. 'Twas the way of the gods. Why, none knew.

Vaidd's mother had delivered nigh unto two hundred pups in her prime, only three of which were female. Obviously Vaidd's three sisters could not mate within their own pack—such caused madness amongst the offspring.

Never had Vaidd heard tell of a Barbarian finding his *vorah* in a sister! Leastways, Nitara, Vala, and Saris had yet to find their true Bloodmates. Even when and if they did, 'twould be another pack's line that his sisters furthered, not his own. Unless, of course, their mates were not of Khan-Gor.

"I have returned from the sleep of the dead," Vaidd rumbled out. His silver eyes were heated, his expression cold and merciless. "With my *vorah*," he growled. Using both hands, he held her naked, unconscious body up like a trophy. He waited for the congratulatory noise to dim before continuing. "As the heir to our clan," he shouted, that all his brothers gathered in the sanctum might hear his voice echoing off the stony, cavern walls, "I have upheld ceremony and waited to join with my Bloodmate until I brought her back to our lair."

His sire nodded his respect of the decision. His brothers hissed theirs. 'Twas not easy for a predator to stay away from the cunt of his mate. The instinctual need to impregnate her had nigh unto overwhelmed Vaidd more than once. The scent of it alone was intoxicating. Holding her naked in his arms had all but driven him mad.

Mayhap 'twas not an accident of nature that Khan-Gori females were so few in number. The average *vorah* could bear up to ten litters throughout her lifetimes. Some, like his mother, bore more, and some less. Should more females come to be, all of them bearing litter after litter of hungry pups, 'twould take an ugly toll on the food chain for a certainty.

And so it was that the mated brother of the pack became the Alpha upon the extinction of their sire's seventh lifetime — even if that brother was not the first-born. Did two brothers within a pack both find their mates — a rarity — the Alpha position was bequeathed to the eldest. Did no brothers of a pack find a mate, again, the Alpha position fell to the eldest. Such was why Vaidd had been named his sire's heir apparent prior to this claiming. When a Barbarian reached his seventh lifetime and none of his sons had mated, 'twas when he formally named his eldest the assumed heir.

Vaidd felt fiercely proud at the offering he was bestowing unto his sire. His father would not join the gods in the Underworld thinking that surely his line was to die off. The she-god of mating had smiled down upon Vaidd. The Zyon bloodline would continue.

Vaidd's sire, Zolak, stood up. His voice was booming, his stance proud. "Let us welcome home your brother — my rightful heir!" he announced. "And let us rejoice at the claiming of his Bloodmate!"

Loud shouts, hisses, and roars filled the sanctum, emotion echoing off the stone walls. Some of the feelings were elation, a triumph that their line would go on. Some of the feelings were akin to despair, for all of the brothers realized 'twas rare for more than one male of the same pack to find a Bloodmate.

Vaidd's hard gaze softened when it landed upon his sister, Nitara. She was so overcome with relief and happiness at Vaidd's good fortune that her eyes had welled up with tears. Nitara and Vaidd had been born of the same litter — the first litter. 'Twas therefore no surprise that their bond had always been a close one.

"Let the claiming begin!" Zolak bellowed, diverting Vaidd's attention back to his sire.

Vaidd cradled his Bloodmate's wee, warm, limp body close to his heart. His fangs couldn't help but to burst out from his gums, so aroused he was. The smell of her skin, the scent of her pussy, urged the animal in him on.

At long last, it was time to claim what was his.

* * * * *

Dot awoke to the sight of hungry gargoyles surrounding her everywhere. She had been strewn out naked on a table, laid in the middle of what looked to be a platter. She knew this was it — sushi city. The only things missing from the scene were an apple in her mouth and various sauces for the wicked beasts to dip her flesh in for their dining pleasure. Instead of chicken nuggets, they'd be getting raw Dot nuggets.

So this is what will become of me? I gave you my last snack cake, you bastard. So much for generosity!

Dot's nostrils flared at the bastard in question. All gargoyles looked alike, but for reasons unknown she could pick her captor out of a line-up that featured one thousand of the things. "I will haunt you from my grave," she ardently vowed. "And I hope I taste like shit!"

One of the gargoyles — not her captor — began speaking. He used words Dot could not understand. All of the gargoyles then joined hands in a circle around her, closed their eyes, and bowed their heads.

Good grief. They had formed a prayer circle around her, no doubt thanking whatever god they worshipped for the bounty they were about to receive! Suddenly she understood what it felt like to be the turkey on Thanksgiving Day.

At least I had enough heart to buy a turkey that was already dead. I hope I give all of you food poisoning and really super bad indigestion!

She hoped they farted her for weeks—a reminder not to go snatch innocent women from their vehicles ever again. And if there was any justice whatsoever in this horrible world of theirs, they'd be belching up Dot nuggets until they took their last breaths.

Dot's mind began to splinter. She felt one small inch away from insanity. This was just too much. The men-beasts with tails had been bad enough. Now she was being prayed over by a pack of gargoyles before they sat down to dine on Dot a l'orange.

She began to scream, a deafening, shrill cry that resonated throughout the stone chamber she'd awoken in and gained everyone's undivided attention. She screamed louder and impossibly more high-pitched.

Their chanting immediately stopped. They began to hiss, all of them except her captor covering their ears. But even he looked ready to pass out.

She'd found a weapon! Oh yes! Oh yes! She just hoped her lungs and vocal chords would comply long enough to get the hell out of here.

Bolting up from her back and onto her feet, Dot stopped screaming and prepared to jump off the table. As soon as her shrieking ceased, the gargoyles all grabbed for her. She screamed again, a piercing sound that made even her wince, as she stood on the platter in a karate "come-get-me-fucker" position. She moved her arms back and forth like an expert in the martial arts anticipating the enemy's next move.

They recovered their ears. She kept up the shrill noise as she jumped off the platter and headed toward the nearest exit.

Where is the way out? I don't need any more complications, God. My lungs are about to implode!

"By the tit of the she-god," one of Vaidd's brothers whimpered, "shut thy wench up!"

"She means to flee from us!" his sire yelled as he kept his sensitive ears covered up. He nodded toward where Vaidd's shrieking Bloodmate was running in circles, desperately trying to find a way out.

Vaidd felt nigh close to swooning from the horrid, deafening noise his *vorah* was making, yet he stumbled as best he could toward her. That, unfortunately, only made her more frantic. Her large, dark eyes widened as she screamed impossibly louder.

'Twas like a kick in the man sac. Vaidd fell to his knees and gasped, trying to regain control of himself that he might regain control of the situation. 'Twas sorely apparent why primitive wenches were hard to tame—or at least one of the reasons why. Verily, they were possessed of wicked defenses. Vaidd grimly realized that his friend Vorik deserved a Khan-Gori medal of valor for the claiming of Nancy.

His eyes narrowing into merciless slits, he forced himself up from his knees and sprang toward his Bloodmate. Her screaming grew worse. But, thank the gods, through gritted teeth and a perspiring brow, he managed to catch her. And then he did something he knew every member of his pack would be forever grateful for—he slapped a palm over her mouth.

The shrieking ceased. All Khan-Gori present breathed a sigh of relief.

* * * * *

This time when they put her on the platter, they tied her down and placed some sort of adhesive that smelled like pinecones over her mouth. Naked, her arms had been hoisted above her head and her legs splayed wide open and secured down. Her ass was at the very end of the platter, almost suspended off the table itself.

As they formed their satanic prayer circle around her once again, Dot realized it was time to give up the ship. She was dead meat and there was no stopping it.

The gargoyles continued to chant, eyes closed, bald heads bowed, to their higher power. She simply couldn't believe this was happening. One minute she'd been heading toward a bachelorette party to sell her sex toys and the next she'd become the main entrée on a gargoyle menu.

Breathing in deeply through her nose, Dot found her courage. They had won, but she would go down with dignity, strength, and pride. (She'd always loved those movies where the fallen hero or heroine died like that.) Yes, she thought wistfully, her life would end on a note of bravery and fortitude. Dorothy Araiza — American heroine extraordinaire. If her people ever found this world and unearthed her skeletal remains, they would surely bury her with eloquent style. Not that it would do her much good because she'd be dead. But oh well, that wasn't the point.

The chanting came to an abrupt halt. The gargoyles lifted their heads and all eyes turned to Dot. Her heartbeat sped up and her gaze widened.

On the other hand, dying with dignity was highly overrated.

Dot began screaming from behind the adhesive, her hands and feet trying to break free from their confinements. She rattled at the ties that bound her, her body shaking and breasts jiggling, all to no avail.

The large, all-encompassing prayer circle broke off into several smaller ones. Ten of the creatures formed the innermost circle around her. Twenty or so creatures formed a circle around them, and so on.

The end was here. Tired and resigned, Dot gave up the good fight and quit squirming. She had raged, she had battled, and she had lost. All good soldiers knew when the hour of doom was upon them. Her last and final hope was that the creatures would show her mercy and knock her out before beginning their dirty deed. Hit her over the head with a hammer, decapitate her — whatever. She just didn't want to be awake for it.

The gargoyles shifted into human forms, making Dot go still. She had thought she'd dreamt that part about her captor — obviously not! She morbidly wondered just why they had bothered shifting into humanoid forms to begin with. One would think it would be easier to tear her apart from limb to limb with claws, talons, and fangs at the ready.

Her captor, the one who had somehow managed to mesmerize her into going willingly into his arms, stood naked and erect between her spread open thighs. Nine other males surrounded her, all of them clothed in that red and black kilt-like skirt with no shirt.

The compulsion to look her vanquisher in the eyes was an overwhelming one. Unlike the last time, Dot now realized it was a form of hypnotism. Knowing what it was, however, didn't make her any better able to resist this time than it had the last.

Her gaze found his. An instant calm stole over her. It felt just like a tranquilizer. When he removed the adhesive from over her mouth, she didn't scream. Instead, the feeling lingered. This time, for whatever reason, she seemed unable to snap out of it. "Han kana," she heard her subjugator murmur. She had no idea what it meant, but the dreamy state that enveloped her kept her from caring.

Two of the clothed males palmed either of Dot's breasts. She felt nothing but pleasure, unable to experience apprehension. They used both of their hands to massage her there, each of them attuned to a single breast. Another set of hands found her arms and massaged them. Another set her legs. Another set her belly. The only part of her that wasn't being intimately stroked was her vagina. Her captor took care of that.

He stroked her pussy softly, sensuously, as their gazes remained locked. He murmured words to her that she didn't comprehend, but that did a number on her hormones.

Dot's breasts were being kneaded in the same gentle, intoxicating manner. Her nipples were pulled at and played with like firm clay in a potter's hands — doing whatever those hands wanted to do with her to elicit the response they were going for. They got it.

She moaned softly, a knot of arousal forming in her belly as the gigantic males worked her body up into a fevered pitch. Her already stiff nipples jutted up further into the air, giving greedy mouths plenty to suck on. She closed her eyes as the feeling of teeth scraping her nipples and enveloping them into hot mouths overwhelmed her. They sucked on her nipples hard while her captor massaged her wet clit, causing her to shiver. Dot cried out, unable to keep herself from responding to the exquisite pleasure.

Something poked at her moist entrance, inducing her eyes to fly open. Him — the one who held the power to mesmerize her — he was trying to get his gigantic cock inside her. Apparently he was accustomed to bedding women with bigger holes, for perspiration dotted his hairline and his jaw was clenched at the effort.

It dawned on her that she should be feeling some sort of apprehension. His cock was HUGE – swollen, erect, and painfully big. She *should* have experienced fear, but she felt nothing but desire for him to be inside of her.

A soft, deep voice in her head kept telling her something, but what Dot had no idea. All she did know was the desire to be impregnated by her subjugator was an overwhelming one.

He rubbed her clit more briskly, making her head fall back on a groan. The mouths on her nipples sucked harder until she was gasping for air and moaning. Her breasts heaved up and down from under their mouths. Her hips instinctively reared up as far as they could given the restraints, pressing her wet flesh against her captor's swollen cock. He hissed as the head slipped in, her pussy enveloping it, holding it in with an unyielding grip.

The erotic body massage at so many hands and mouths was beyond anything. The mouths sucked her nipples harder. Her captor's thumb rubbed her clit faster. She could hear how wet she was, the sticky sound of her pussy being massaged reaching her ears.

"Oh God," Dot breathed out. *"I'm coming."*

She came loudly, violently, the intense coil in her belly springing loose. "Oh—*ooooooh!*" Blood rushed to her nipples and face, heating them. Her entire body convulsed, shaking. Unable to move, all she could do was lie there and groan like a dying animal.

He impaled her cunt in one smooth thrust, turning her groan into a whimper. She felt the pain, but couldn't experience the fear that should have accompanied it—the situation was akin to losing one's virginity while heavily intoxicated.

Fangs burst from his gums as he threw his head back on a roar of victory and possessiveness. The males surrounding them hissed and growled, all of their fangs baring, all of their silver eyes turning a haunting blood-red.

Dot couldn't look away from her captor's jugular vein to save herself. *What the hell is happening to me?* The compulsion to bite it, to taste his blood, was powerful. She couldn't blink, couldn't do anything besides lie there and want what she couldn't reach.

Her hands sprang free from the binds. Her legs were loosed next.

Their gazes clashed.

Still buried inside her to the hilt, her captor leaned over her comparatively tiny body and, looking to the side, bared his neck to her. Dot wouldn't understand the force that drew her to that gorgeous vein until much later, but she didn't care either. She just wanted it.

Wrapping her arms around his neck, she closed her eyes and sank her teeth into his jugular. He hissed and groaned in animalistic pleasure. Her human teeth were not able to tear through it, but were sufficiently strong to clamp it together — and pinch just hard enough to squeeze a few droplets of blood from his neck.

The sweet droplets of blood touched her tongue. Instinctively, she let her arms fall away from his neck. Arching her breasts up like an offering, she bared her neck to the half man half gargoyle.

He didn't go for her jugular, damn it! And though her human mind was wary in the deepest recesses of its consciousness, oh how her body wanted him to. Her womb repeatedly contracted at the mere thought of such. But, no, he wasn't ready. His deadly fangs grazed just above her heart instead, causing a few droplets of her blood to spill out. His tongue darted out, sensually lapping them up.

Dot screamed, the orgasm sudden and ruthless. He growled as she convulsed, her moans and blood an aphrodisiac.

He began to fuck her, pumping in and out of her cunt in long, territorial thrusts. She groaned, the scent of their combined arousal and the sound of her pussy suctioning in his cock on every outstroke a turn-on.

"Fuck her harder, Vaidd," one male purred.

"Your wife wants it harder," another one growled.

It occurred to Dot they were calling her his—her captor's—*wife!* It also dawned on her that she could understand what was being said. Words, once foreign, now infiltrated her entire being as native. She was given no time to figure out why.

"I am Vaidd," her vanquisher murmured, his teeth gritting from the tightness of her pussy. "And you," he said roughly, "are mine."

He fucked her harder, going primal on her, riding her body like he meant to brand every inch of her as his. Her tits jiggled with every thrust, moans pulled from her lips as though he was getting his wish. His eyes were fully crimson, fangs bared as he growled and roared out his pleasure.

"Oh God!" Dot screamed, her head falling back. Her eyes closed in an ecstasy she'd never before experienced. *"Yesssssss!"*

He pumped her cunt harder — faster — deeper — *more, more, more.*

In and out.

Over and over.

Again and again and again.

Sweat-slick skin slapped against sweat slick-skin. Her stiff nipples were further sensitized with every jiggle brought on by every of his thrusts. His jaw clenched as he fucked her, teeth gritting as he possessively sank his cock into her.

"I'm coming!" Dot groaned, her eyelids flying open. And this time she wanted that jugular when she came. She didn't know why she wanted it, only that her body was commanding her to bite it.

Baring her human teeth on a snarl to rival one of Vaidd's, Dot wrapped her arms around his neck and bit down. He roared out his pleasure, then, still fucking her, sank his fangs into her jugular as she clamped down onto his. Vaidd's blood hit her tongue, Dot's blood gushed onto his.

The mutually experienced orgasm was all-consuming, shattering, in its depths. Their mouths broke free in order to moan as both of them shook from the violence of it. Hot cum erupted, filling her insides. Blood trickled down her neck. They groaned and held each other tightly, riding out wave after delicious wave of erotic synergy.

When it was over, when both of their breathing had returned to a semi-normal state, Vaidd slowly withdrew his still-erect cock from Dot's flesh on a suctioning sound. Panting, he looked down into her eyes and laid her fully on her back as he released her from the spell that had enveloped her.

His eyes returned to silver with black pupils, flicking over her face, memorizing her features. "What is thy name, *zya*?" he purred.

Zya—little one.

"Dot," she whispered. Her brown eyes widened on a plethora of questions. But she decided to get out the most pressing one. "Does this mean you don't plan to eat me?" she squeaked. Dot couldn't imagine anyone making love to her like that, giving her the mother of all orgasms, only to turn her into gargoyle-chow. Not to mention the fact that the emotions radiating from him were almost overwhelming in their protective possessiveness. Still, she supposed anything could happen in a world like this.

Vaidd's gaze narrowed in incomprehension, then sparkled in mischievous understanding. "I'll eat you for a certainty, but not like that."

He didn't smile as the other members in the chamber began to boom with laughter, but his eyes were dancing and his purr was comforting.

"Well, that's a relief," she said dumbly. *I mean, really, what does one say in a situation like this!* She made to sit up. "Why can I understand what you're saying now, and vice versa, when I couldn't before? Why did you lay me on a platter if you didn't mean to eat me? And what in the world were those tailed things that dragged me into the cave? They had tails, okay! Oh and—"

He pressed two fingers gently against her lips. "In a sennight I shall answer all thy questions," he murmured.

A sennight! Thanks to all of the historical romance novels she'd read over the years, she realized what he meant. But, "Why a week?"

"Because."

She frowned. Wordy he was not. "Because why?"

He grunted. "Because 'tis time for my wee love to evolve." He motioned toward her legs.

Dot glanced down. She gasped in shock and more than a little fright. A sticky web-like substance was steadily encasing her feet...and crawling up higher to encase her everywhere. She screamed, beyond horrified, as she watched the web climb higher and higher and higher. Her heartbeat thumped wildly as it spread to her arms and her chest and—

"You shall be cocooned but a sennight, my love. Then you shall be of my species."

What a comfort!

"Why are you doing this to me?" Dot howled as the web began crawling up to encase her face. "A woman gives you snack cakes and you put her in a web!" The last part of her sentence was mumbled out as the web closed over her mouth.

Arrrrrg!

Chapter Seven

One week later

Vaidd paced as he waited and waited for his *vorah* to hatch. His cock was nigh unto stone it was so aching and swollen from this last sennight without her.

"Son," Zolak rumbled out, "take you a walk. Go hunt. Do something to distract thyself. Verily, you are driving the pack daft with the pacing. She will hatch when the metabolic changes within have fully occurred and not a moment before. This you know!"

He ran a hand over his jaw, sighing. His sire was correct and, as he'd said, he knew it. Glancing up to the *vorah-sac* suspended deep within the Zyon stronghold, he looked away and nodded his agreement. "Aye," he murmured. "I shall go for a walk."

There was more to his anxiety than a desire to mate, but Vaidd would not share feelings of the heart with his father. Namely, the scared, helpless manner in which Dot had last looked upon Vaidd before being cocooned nigh unto tore his heart clean out. He wanted her to hatch so she'd realize he would never hurt her, leave her, or in any way endanger her.

She was his—now and always. He could never do anything to harm her.

"Go, son," Zolak said softly, knowingly. "She will hatch before you know it."

He inclined his head and then walked away.

* * * * *

Air rushed into Dot's lungs, filling them. Her eyes flew open, fangs bursting from her gums. Claws shot out from her fingers and toes, spikes jutted up, forming a wristband of deadly pikes around either hand.

He was near. Her one.

The need to be impregnated overpowered her, beckoned to her, made every egg in her ovaries tingle. Dot shredded her cocoon faster than a great white shark could gulp a tuna and took to the air.

I'm flying! Oh dear lord I am flying!

The human memory cells in her brain were wary, but the primitive need to fill her womb with Vaidd's pups overrode everything. She was so horny she couldn't stand it, felt like she'd go insane if he didn't impale her and fuck her like the animal she now was.

She flew out of the cave and over a nearby stream. The scent of food momentarily distracted her. Swooping down, she snarled at her prey and, snatching it up from the icy water below, tore both heads off some sort of fish and gobbled it down.

Oh God, I've just eaten a two-headed fish! While. It. Was. Alive. Ohhhh noooooo!

A palm tragically lifting to her forehead, Dot's wings swooped with less and less vigor, until finally, she was on the ground. Glancing at her reflection in the stream, she felt the drama queen lance right through her.

I'm bald! I ate a two-headed fish while it was still alive and now I am bald!

Only whilst in kor-tari form, a deep voice answered in her mind. *And you are gorgeous in both forms to me.*

Dot's bald, silver head came up. Horniness returned as she saw Vaidd swooping down from the air. There went those damn eggs tingling again.

Well, she sniffed in her mind, *if I'm gorgeous to you then I suppose —*

He was on her in a heartbeat, covering her from behind, ready to fuck her. He growled her into submission, fangs bared as he took her down to her knees. She growled back — mostly just because she could and it felt kinda neat — then pressed her swollen pussy up into the air so he count mount her.

Vaidd sank into her flesh from behind, howling at the exquisite feel of her tight cunt enveloping and gripping his cock. He thrust into her to the hilt, then rode her hard, wasting no time in taking what he considered to be his.

"Yesss," Dot hissed. She glanced at him from over her shoulder and snarled. *"Fuck me harder."*

"Like this?" Vaidd growled, sinking deep into her cunt, over and over, again and again. He scratched at the sensitive skin of her hips with his claws, making her keen in pleasure. "Does my little one like it rough?"

Oh yes, Dot thought. She hadn't known she'd liked to be taken so animalistically prior to her evolution, but now there was no going back. And the hip thing...who knew?

"Scratch me harder! Fuck me harder! Get me pregnant!"

She didn't know what she wanted more — all of them. She was lost in a delirious haze of pleasure, wanting everything and anything her mate could give her.

Vaidd picked up the pace of their joining, hissing as he rooted inside her. He scratched her hips harder, fucked her harder—everything harder. He slammed into her cunt again and again, merciless in his domination.

And then he gave her his babies.

On a piercing roar, Vaidd lowered his head to his *vorah's* neck and sank his teeth deep inside the sweet, warm vein. She howled as she came, her entire body bucking and convulsing from the pleasure of it. Vaidd followed quickly behind, sinking into her cunt as fast and deep as he could, then spurting his seed deep into her pussy.

He wasn't done with his Bloodmate. Not even close.

By the time Vaidd picked up his wife and flew with her in his arms back to their lair, he had fucked her eight times. There was no question to Dot as to whether or not fertilization had occurred. She had known the second it had happened. A warm feeling, half primitive and half enlightened in nature, had engulfed her.

Life already grew in her belly.

* * * * *

They lay next to each other within the stronghold of the Zyon pack in humanoid form. Vaidd ran a callused hand through her chestnut-brown hair, his silver eyes all over her naked body. Seeing her gargoyle as a man didn't, surprisingly enough, make Dot go all shy on him this time. The feelings inside her were impossible to explain to a human brain, she realized, but they were there.

Completion. Elation. A knowing. Like this really was the one and only. There could never be another male of any species that would make her heart ache with joy and love like Vaidd did.

But the human memories that still dwelled within were confused and wary. They didn't understand this newfound passion, didn't comprehend how she could love someone she'd just met so fully and completely. Like she'd die without him near her.

"What are you thinking?" he murmured, his gaze coming up to meet hers.

Dot blew out a breath. How could she explain this? "I hardly know you," she muttered. "I just don't understand why I'm feeling like I am."

One side of his mouth slowly lifted into a mischievous grin. God, he was handsome. Everything she'd ever asked for in a man but never thought she'd have. "'Tis my wicked big cock."

Or almost everything, she thought on a grunt. "I'm being serious."

"I know." He sighed, the universal sound of a man who didn't feel like exploring the how and the why, just accepting things as is. But, to his credit, he explored them with her anyway. "The longer we are together, the more you will understand. 'Tis no way for me to explain it, *zya*. Not really."

That she could believe. "Do you feel confused too?"

"Nay."

"Why not?"

He shrugged. "I've grown up this way my entire life. I've got nothing to look back on and compare it against." He didn't smile, he rarely did that, but his eyes were on fire. "You are my one, my only," he murmured. "There could never be another for me."

That did things to her heart she couldn't begin to describe. How a spinster like her could end up with a gorgeous man like this—who wanted only her no less!—was beyond wonderful. And better yet, she felt the same way about him.

"I feel the same way," she said on a soft smile. "And yet the confusion remains."

"One day there will be no confusion. One day all parts of your mind will accept what is true."

That sounded so arrogant. And yet she knew he was right. What's more, it's exactly what she needed to hear.

"Lay thy head down upon me, *vorah*," Vaidd commanded, yawning. When she complied, he squeezed her affectionately. "We've six entire lives together. All will be well. On the morrow we can talk more of this."

"Six lives?" she said excitedly, her head bobbing up. "But how can—"

He grunted as he placed a gentle finger to her lips. "Verily, the god of speech did not overlook you when handing out things to say."

She frowned. He grinned.

Dot's heart sped up. He had a beautiful smile.

"On the morrow then," she said, imitating his words. She loved the way it made her sound all British! "We can talk then."

* * * * *

Vaidd awoke to the feel of his Bloodmate licking his stiff cock. He sucked in a breath, his stomach muscles clenching, as he watched her go down on him. Her eyes were closed, a dreamy smile on her face, as she nigh unto suckled him blind.

He swallowed heavily. The stories of primitive females were true. Native Khan-Gori females would never think to do such a thing in so far as he was aware. Only the female yenni would suckle a Barbarian.

Catching her hair and holding it away from her face so as not to impede his view, Vaidd's eyelids grew heavy as he watched Dot's warm, suctioning mouth work up and down the length of his manhood. She sucked on him slowly, savoring him as though his cock was a favorite treat.

His balls were so tight they felt ready to explode.

"That's it," he said hoarsely, "love me with your mouth, little one." His toes curled as he watched her take him in, the sound of saliva meeting hard flesh further arousing him.

"Mmmm," Vaidd purred, lying back on an elbow. He guided her head with his hand, indicating he wanted suckled faster.

Dot met his challenge, fulfilled his desire. She sucked on his cock faster, her head bobbing up and down with the effort.

Vaidd hissed out his pleasure, his balls getting impossibly tighter. His jaw clenched and his teeth gritted as he watched his wife suck him off, suctioning his cock into her throat over and over, again and again.

"Dot."

He burst on a loud growl that resonated throughout their lair. His cum spurted up, and she was quick to drink of him. Dot lapped at him with more proficiency than any female yenni, even sucking the hole at the tip to make sure not a single drop of his essence had been missed.

His breathing was labored as her head slowly came up. An eyebrow rose at the devilish look on her face. "Aye?" he panted.

She licked her lips, making him gulp. Never had he seen a woman of any species so sexy as this one. "Now that I've got you just like I want you…" Dot tantalizingly climbed up on his chest and stretched her gorgeous body out on him. "I've got a few questions that the speech god gave me to ask you."

Vaidd threw his head back and laughed. A twinkle in his eye, he grabbed both well-rounded cheeks on her backside and kneaded them like the treasures they were. "Ask away. I would never wish to displease the speech god."

Epilogue

Vaidd had answered all of Dot's questions that morning in their lair. And oh boy had she had quite a few! She smiled at the memory as she sat on the floor with her first litter — a son and two daughters — and taught the adorable three-year-old pups how to shape-shift.

"*Vazi,*" her daughter, Nitara, inquired. Nitara had been named for Vaidd's favored sister. "When will papa be home?"

"Aye, when, *vazi*?" her two other pups chirped in.

Dot smiled, unadulterated happiness enveloping her every single time one of her babies called her *vazi* — mommy. She sometimes had to pinch herself to remind her human memories that this wasn't all a dream.

Vaidd, she conceded, had been right when he'd told her that one day her mind would fully accept the truth for what it was. It hadn't taken long. Maybe — oh…a whole day!

"He'll be home soon," she promised. He'd only been gone an hour, long enough to go barter for some of her favorite candies from the local merchant. He planned to trade two female yenni for a six-months supply. Why? She was pregnant again and Vaidd had found during the first litter that the candies in question were her favorites. "Now don't you want to surprise papa by showing off how good you are at shape-shifting?"

Nitara popped the thumb out of her mouth. "Nay." Her piece spoken, she popped it back in. Dot could only giggle.

By the time Vaidd returned, his pups were ready to pounce, and pounce they did. Dot stayed on the floor, smiling as she watched her Bloodmate play with them, wondering why it was that human bonds never fully developed to the extent that Khan-Gori ones did. The babies couldn't stand for *either* parent to be out of their sight. Usually human children preferred one parent's presence to the other.

Khan-Gor, as it turned out, was a pretty fascinating place to live. A medieval realm in some ways—especially in terms of fashion and how the caved cities and marketplaces looked. A primitive realm in other ways—especially in terms of the whole drinking each other's blood and hunting dinner for yourself thing. And a technologically advanced realm in yet other ways—especially in terms of the weaponry and space-traveling ships that could be found here. Khan-Gor was yin and yang, ancient and advanced, modern and a throwback.

It was perfection.

Well, Dorothy, there's no place like home…

This *was* her home, the large cave-lair that boasted thirty chambers, a vast dining hall, and a world of comfort. This *was* her family, the babies and husband that she loved so much. She couldn't imagine life without them, and didn't want to either.

Later, after the pups had been fed and put to bed, Vaidd turned to Dot with those smoldering, blazing eyes of his. She rose to her feet and held her arms up to the giant. He picked her up so she could wrap her arms around his neck and kiss him like he'd never been kissed before.

"I love you," she whispered against his mouth.

He gave her an affectionate squeeze. "And I love you, my little one."

Their tongues danced and dueled, and before long Vaidd was hard as a rock. Dot purred into his mouth, rubbing her pussy against his erection. Not one to miss a mating moment, her Bloodmate carried her to their bedchamber and laid her on the soft animal hides so that he could love her properly.

"You have that devilish twinkle in your eyes, my love," Vaidd murmured as he settled himself on top of her.

She grinned. That's because she loved sex. Lots and lots of sweaty, pumping, pounding, gloriously wicked, undeniably naughty, kinky as all hell S-E-X with a capital S for *Sex*. And, she conceded, because she loved him and would be forever grateful to whatever power brought her to this place. Oh and there was one other reason for the devilish twinkle in her eyes, too…

"Well," she said in her Marilyn Monroe whisper, "I was thinking we could get a little kinky tonight."

Vaidd grunted. He slashed a definitive hand through the air. "Nay. There will be no shoving one of those toys of yours up my arse this eve." He sniffed. "I'm not in the mood. Leastways, not now."

Dot chuckled. He loved her latest invention, "Annie-In-My-Arse", and he damn well knew it. Annie had developed quite a few devoted fans in the merchant stalls for a reason. Dot was certain her husband would be in the mood before long. But for now…

"I love you," Dot breathed out as Vaidd sank into her welcoming, tight flesh. Oh how she loved him!

"I love you, too, *zya*," Vaidd whispered between kisses to her neck. He lifted his head and smiled. "Now and forever, you are my one and only." His sexy, light brown eyebrows rose. "Even if you do like putting wicked toys up your Bloodmate's arse."

To Be Continued...

In

NEVER A SLAVE

Made in the USA
San Bernardino, CA
18 July 2018